All rights reserved under International and Pan-American Copyright Conventions.
Published in the United States by Listening Library, a division of Random House, Inc.
Distributed by Random House, Inc., New York.
Listening Library is a registered trademark of Random House, Inc.

As adapted by Mark Sottnick for the video version
of *The Night Before Christmas* narrated by Meryl Streep

Executive Producers:
Rabbit Ears Entertainment LLC
Chris Campbell & Mark Sottnick

Design by Susan Daulton

www.listeninglibrary.com

Book manufactured in China. CD mastered in Hong Kong.

Library of Congress Cataloging in Publication Data
Moore, Clement, C., 1779-1863. The Night Before Christmas. Summary: a well-known poem
about an important Christmas Eve visitor.   1. Santa Claus—Juvenile poetry   2. Children's
poetry, American.   3. Christmas—Juvenile poetry   4. Santa Claus—Poetry.
5. Christmas—Poetry.   I. Cone, William, ill.   II. Title. PS2429.M5 N5 1992   [Fic]
92-022712   ISBN 0-8870-8260-2   ISBN-13: 978-0-7393-3699-1 (book/compact disc)
ISBN-10: 0-7393-3699-1 (book/compact disc)

10   9   8   7   6   5   4   3   2   1

The
Night
Before
Christmas

Written by
Clement C. Moore

Illustrated by
William Cone

T was the night before Christmas, when all through the house
Not a creature was stirring, not even a mouse;
The stockings were hung by the chimney with care,
In hopes that St. Nicholas soon would be there;

1

The children were nestled all snug in their beds
While visions of sugar-plums danced in their heads;

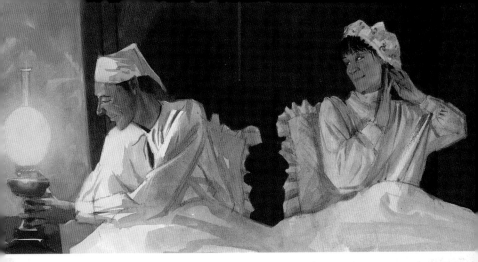

And Mamma in her kerchief, and I in my cap,

Had just settled in for a long winter's nap

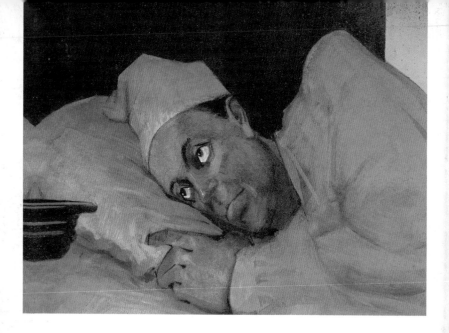

When out on the lawn there arose such a clatter,
I sprang from my bed to see what was the matter.
Away to the window I flew like a flash,
Tore open the shutters and threw up the sash.

The moon on the breast of the new-fallen snow
Gave the luster of midday to objects below,
When, what to my wondering eyes should appear,
But a miniature sleigh, and eight tiny reindeer,

With a little old driver, so lively and quick,
I knew in a moment it must be St. Nick.

More rapid than eagles his coursers they came,

And he whistled, and shouted, and called them by name:

Now, Dasher! now, Dancer!
now, Prancer and Vixen!
On Comet! on Cupid!
on, Donner and Blitzen!
To the top of the porch!
to the top of the wall!
now dash away! dash away!
dash away all!

As dry leaves that before the wild hurricane fly,
When they meet with an obstacle, mount to the sky,
So up to the house-top the coursers they flew,
With the sleigh full of toys, and St. Nicholas, too.

And then, in a twinkling, I heard on the roof
The prancing and pawing of each little hoof.
As I drew in my head, and was turning around,
Down the chimney St. Nicholas came with a bound.

He was dressed all in fur, from his head to his foot,
And his clothes were all tarnished with ashes and soot;
A bundle of toys he had flung on his back,
And he looked like a peddler just opening his pack.

His eyes how they twinkled! his dimples how merry!
His cheeks were like roses, his nose like a cherry!
His droll little mouth was drawn up like a bow,
And the beard of his chin was as white as the snow;

The stump of a pipe he held tight in his teeth,
And the smoke it encircled his head like a wreath;
He had a broad face and a little round belly,
That shook when he laughed, like a bowlful of jelly.

He was chubby and plump
a right jolly old elf,
And I laughed when I
    saw him,
in spite of myself;
A wink of his eye
and a twist of his head
Soon gave me to know
I had nothing to dread.

He spoke not a word, but went straight to his work,
And filled all the stockings; then turned with a jerk,
And laying his finger aside of his nose,
And giving a nod, up the chimney he rose;

He sprang to his sleigh,
to his team gave a whistle,
And away they all flew
like the down of a thistle.
But I heard him exclaim,
ere he drove out of sight,

Happy Christmas to All and to All a Good Night!

READ ME A STORY

Did you know that hearing books read aloud is
critical to developing a child's reading skills?

Whether it is snuggling up at bedtime with a book, taking
a 20 minute reading break during a busy day or
playing an audiobook on the next family car ride, sharing
good stories with a child is key to instilling the love of reading.

To find out more about how audiobooks can play an important role in
your child's education, visit our website at www.listeninglibrary.com

---

The Starbucks Foundation's Giving Voice grants fund programs for youth
that integrate literacy with personal and civic action. Starbucks believes
literacy begins with the mastery of basic skills for the purpose of personal
and civic transformation. For information on Starbucks Foundation,
visit www.starbucks.com/aboutus/foundation.asp

"We believe the words of a child
who has learned to read, or the words
of a family finding enrichment
in new opportunity, are the reasons
to give back and to give more."
—Howard Schultz
Chairman
Starbucks Coffee Company

Perk up your ears and savor a great story!

Rabbit Ears stories are true classics of children's literature that have delighted and entertained countless families.

Now available to a new generation, these favorites have been brought to life by some of Hollywood's biggest stars and an array of talented and award-winning musicians.

For more information visit us online at
randomhouse.com/audio/rabbitears

Listening Library is pleased to be the exclusive publisher of Rabbit Ears® audio programs.